CAPTAIN AMERICA

AN ORIGIN STORY

Bath · New York · Cologne · Melbourne · Delhi
Hong Kong · Shenzhen · Singapore · Amsterdam

This edition published by Parragon Books Ltd in 2015

Parragon Books Ltd
Chartist House
15–17 Trim Street
Bath BA1 1HA, UK
www.parragon.com

ISBN 978-1-4723-8172-9

Printed in China

Before you were born – in fact, long before even the oldest person you know had been born – a peaceful little island sat right off the mainland of a place that was called different things by all the different nations of people who lived there.

As time went on, more and more
people came to this little island.

They wanted to leave behind the lives
they led in a place they called the Old World ...

... and build new ones in a place where
they believed anything was possible.

People came from all over the world.
For most, this island was the first stop
on the path to a new life in this young nation.

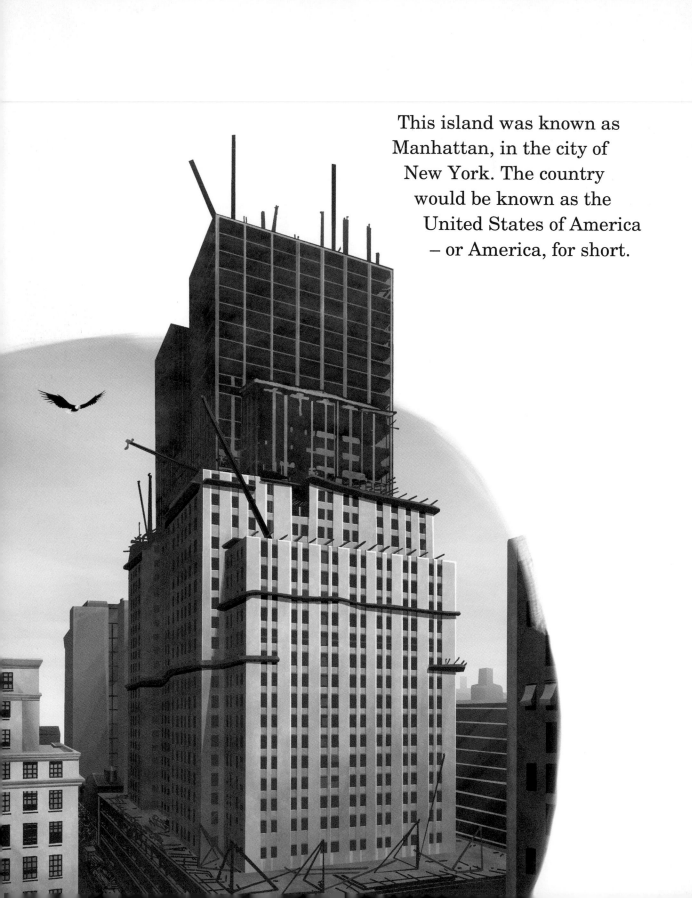

This island was known as
Manhattan, in the city of
New York. The country
would be known as the
United States of America
– or America, for short.

Before America was even two hundred years old ...

... it was called upon to fight alongside other countries in a terrible war that was destroying the world.

The news of war moved people.

It seemed like everyone in the country
wanted to join the army to help.

Including a young man named Steve Rogers.

Steve had been upset about the war for some time. Now that America was involved, he could finally do something about it.

Soon, Steve was in a long line of men waiting to be examined. If the men passed, they would be sent to the war.

Steve waited
his turn.

Every man so
far had passed.

Steve was
confident he
would, too.

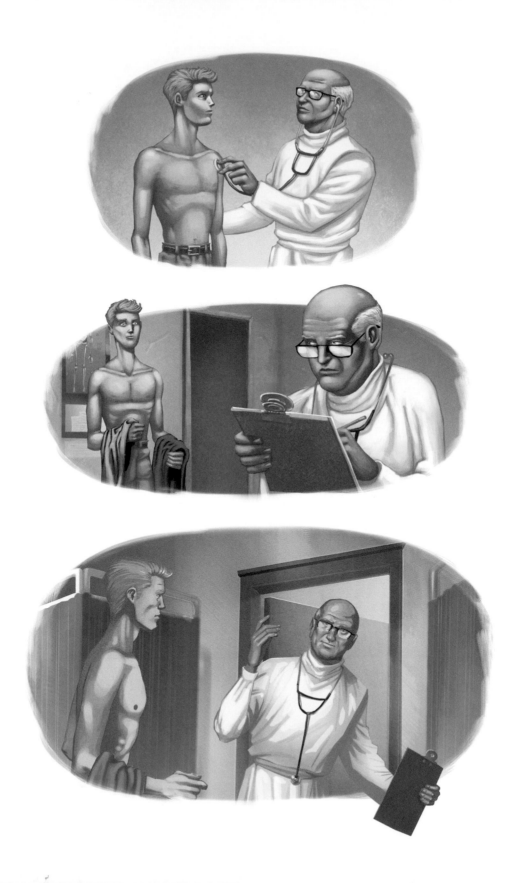

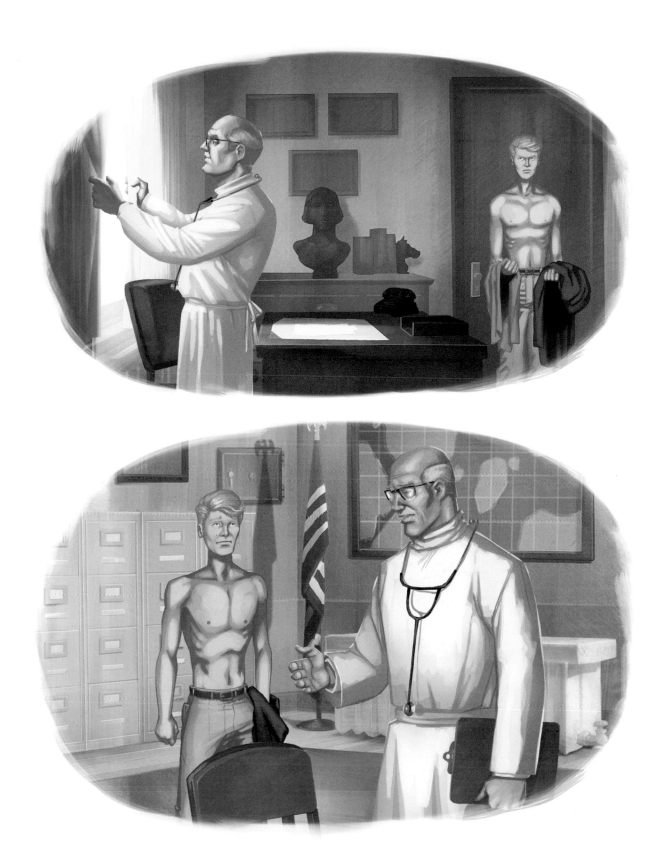

The doctor told Steve that he was in no shape to join the army.

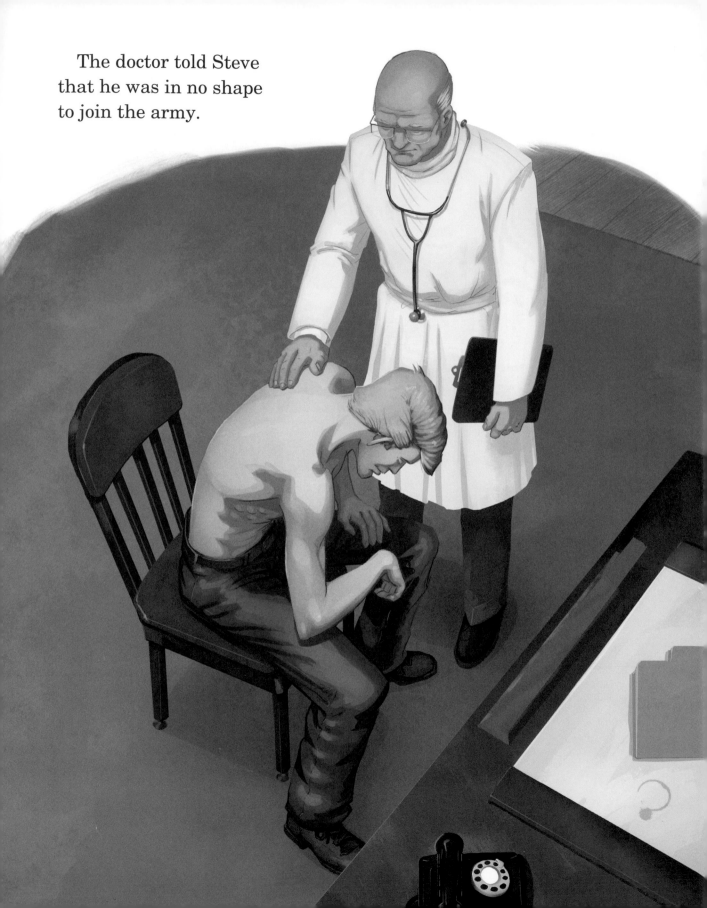

But then he told him there was another way to get into the army. He handed Steve a file marked

CLASSIFIED – PROJECT: REBIRTH.

The doctor told Steve that if the experiment worked, he would be able to join the army. Steve said he would try anything to become a soldier.

The doctor called in a general named Chester Phillips. General Phillips was in charge of Project: Rebirth.

The general led Steve down a
hidden hallway to a secret exit.

Soon, the two men were crossing
the bridge into nearby Brooklyn.

They arrived at
an antiques shop
in a run-down,
dangerous-looking
area. An old woman
let them in and led
them downstairs.

But the shop was not an antiques shop at all!
It was a cover for an underground lab.

And the owner was not an
old woman, but a secret agent!

General Phillips introduced Steve to
the project's lead scientist, Doctor Erskine.

He told Steve that the Super-Soldier serum ...

... combined with the Vita-Rays ...

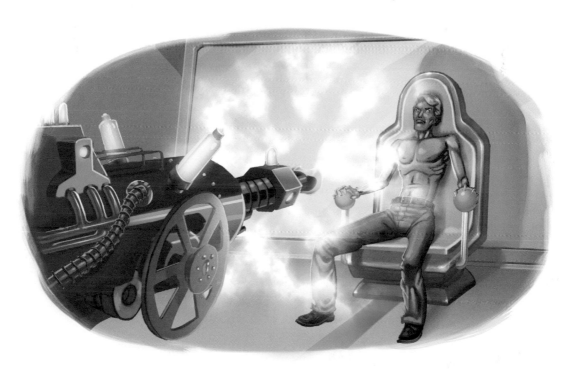

... would transform
him from frail and
sickly Steve Rogers ...

... into America's
FIRST AVENGER!

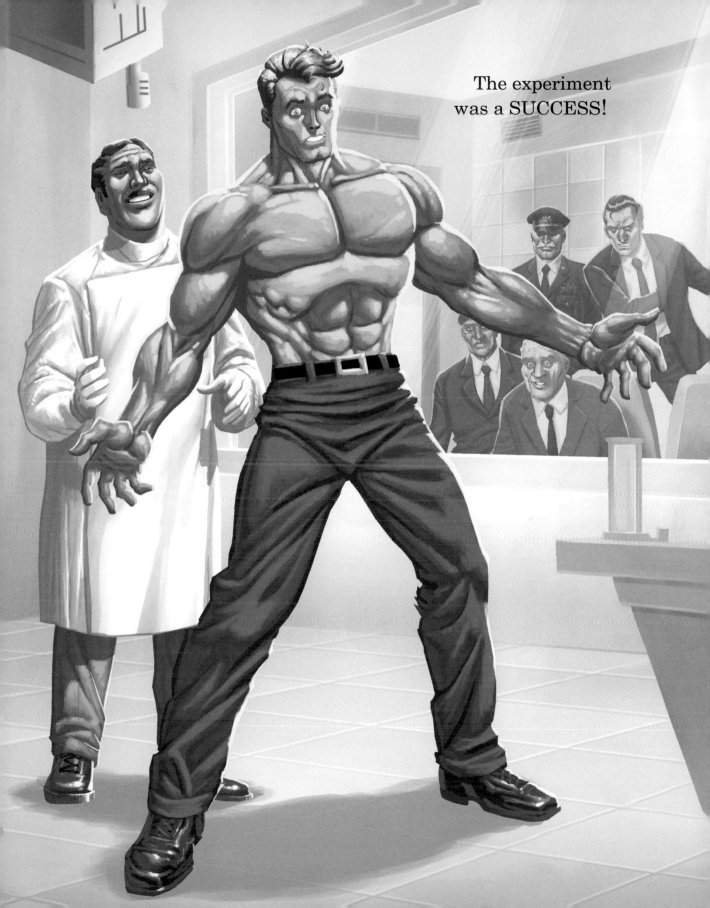

But before Steve, General Phillips or anyone else in the lab could notice, an enemy spy who had been working in the lab attacked!

He did not want the Americans to have such power!

The doctor was hurt and unable to duplicate the serum.

But Steve, in his
new Super-Soldier
body, was safe ...

... and he was angry!

The army put Steve through a special training
camp to teach him how to use his new body.

The general presented Steve with a special shield made of the strongest known metal and a unique costume to help Steve mask his identity.

With the costume and shield, Steve would now be known as America's most powerful soldier ...

... CAPTAIN AMERICA!

Captain America's missions were often dangerous.

In order to keep his secret safe, the general asked Steve to pretend to be a clumsy army private.

But when no one was looking, Steve put on his costume and fought for justice.

Steve's reputation as a clumsy guy meant he was often transferred.

But Steve's moving around allowed Captain America to fight on many different fronts of the worldwide war!

No one ever suspected that the worst private in the US Army was also the best soldier that the army had!

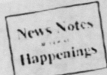

Captain America kept on
fighting for liberty, until finally ...

... THE WAR HAD BEEN WON!

Though the country might not always live up to its promises, as long as Steve was able, he vowed to protect it and its ideals: justice, equality, freedom ...

THE
ORIGINAL
NEW
YORKERS

... and the dream of what the
nation he loved could accomplish.